Blacktooth's Treasure Chest

The Adventures of Blacktooth the Pirate

Jay S. Willis

Arcanitium Press

Copyright © 2020 by **Jay S. Willis**

All rights reserved. No part of this publication may be reproduced, distributed, or transmitted in any form or by any means, without prior written permission.

Jay S. Willis/Arcanitium Press
P.O. Box 85
610 Gay St.
Portsmouth, Ohio 45662
www.jayswillis.net

Publisher's Note: This is a work of fiction. Names, characters, places, and incidents are a product of the author's imagination. Locales and public names are sometimes used for atmospheric purposes. Any resemblance to actual people, living or dead, or to businesses, companies, events, institutions, or locales is completely coincidental.

Book Layout © 2020 BookDesignTemplates.com
Cover Illustration by Duketranart

Blacktooth's Treasure Chest/ Jay S. Willis. -- 1st ed.
ISBN: 978-1-7359243-0-4

Dedicated to Jordan I. Willis

Brought to you by the letter "P".

Contents

Marooned 7
Survival 11
Broken Skull Island 13
Riddles 23
Treasure 29
Pirate Name 35
Blacktooth's Treasure Chest 39
ABOUT THE AUTHOR 45
Acknowledgements 47
SNEAK PEEK 49
   Blacktooth and the Legend of Skull Mountain 49
Books by The Author 53

6   Jay S. Willis

Chapter One

Marooned

Blacktooth the Pirate held onto the mast of his ship for dear life. The skull and crossbones flag flapped wildly above his head while the waves crashed a few feet below. He didn't want to go down with the ship. He had never thought much of that idea even though other captains said it was part of The Pirate Code. This was one rule he intended to break.

He hoped to make it ashore to the island in the distance without the sharks eating him. Death by sharks was not his idea of fun, and neither was having your ship sunk.

Getting to the island was going to be a bit of a challenge since Blacktooth didn't know how to swim. In fact, he was terrified of water. This, of course, was a little-known fact about Blacktooth. It wouldn't do for the other pirates to learn he was afraid of anything, especially water. They would all tease him mercilessly if they found out.

The ship sank lower and lower as the sun slowly melted into the horizon like a dollop of butter on a hot baked potato. Blacktooth was famished since he hadn't yet had dinner. By nightfall, he was treading water as he struggled to hold on to the flagpole a few feet above water level. It looked as if Blacktooth's life as a pirate was about to end.

Just when he believed all hope lost, he spied something bobbing on the waves. Either a giant square fish was swimming toward him, or the hideously pink armoire he had "borrowed" from the Queen of Zithromaz floated to his rescue.

A few minutes and several splinters later, Blacktooth the Pirate perched atop a huge pink dresser filled with exotic clothing like a lonely flamingo on a log in the middle of the ocean. Confidence filled Blacktooth and he believed he could make it to the island now if he could find a way to paddle the dresser ashore. He opened the left-hand door looking for anything of use. The door came off the hinges, which was just as well; he could use it as a paddle.

After about two hours, Blacktooth paddled his way to the tiny island. Overjoyed to be on land again, he bent over and kissed the ground. Now Blacktooth was soaking wet and his face was caked with sand, but he wasn't shark food. It was a good day after all.

The night breeze blew along the island's beach and Blacktooth shivered from the chill. Though he knew he looked silly, Blacktooth donned most of the Queen's exotic clothing. He'd stay warmer that way, at least until he could build a fire.

It took quite a while for him to find enough wood and rocks, but he never gave up and managed to get a fire started. In the process of scouring the beach, Blacktooth found several planks from his ship washed onto the shore. By morning, he hoped some of his clothes, gold, or other treasures might make their way to the island. Some food would be nice too. Thinking about Cookie Carl's barbecue burgers and onion rings made his stomach rumble.

Chapter Two

Survival

He wasn't worried terribly about his crew. Those scurvy savages had abandoned ship on the lifeboats, so he knew they were safe somewhere.

Blacktooth's stomach roared and growled like an angry bear until he realized he hadn't eaten for way too long. Luckily, this island had trees full of fruit and bushes dripping with berries dotting the landscape as far as he could see. After some foraging, Blacktooth sat down by the fire and enjoyed a nice meal of seared pineapples which he skewered on wispy branches he found in the underbrush, raw bananas, coconut milk, and berries.

The next thing he knew, the sun peeked over the horizon. He smiled at the fact he'd survived long enough to see another morning. As he'd hoped, many things from the ship washed ashore. The best thing he found was his wooden toolbox. Blacktooth figured he might be stuck on the island a while but with his tools he could build a shelter.

The first few days, the time Blacktooth did not spend gathering food, he began constructing a small hut. He had plenty of good wood from the torn and tattered hull of his once beautiful ship. Seeing huge hunks of the *Crusty Claw* on the beach made him sad, but at least he had survived.

Chapter Three

Broken Skull Island

He should have known it would happen. Blacktooth was one of the best-known pirates and many others, not on his crew, were jealous. After years of sailing the high seas with other pirates like Greasy Hook, Red Patch McGee, and Peg Leg Morgan, Blacktooth decided it was time to make a name for himself and he was one of the youngest captains to own a ship..

Back then, he wasn't known as Blacktooth. You didn't earn your pirate name until you did something bold and daring. Back then, Blacktooth was plain, old Bart Baker, a rather boring name as pirate names go.

Bart had saved up a lot of money working for Peg Leg Morgan. Old Peg Leg decided he was about ready to retire and agreed to sell Bart his ship, The *Crusty Claw*, on one condition. Bart had to earn his pirate name first. If he did that, he would have a ship and a crew to go along with it.

All Bart had to do was figure out a way to be bold and daring enough to earn his pirate name. Bart continued traveling with Old Peg Leg for several months to find any way he could to earn his name. Finally, Bart had an idea while looking through a book he'd just purchased in a small shop at Port Seabreeze. Pirates don't usually like reading books, but Bart was the exception. He loved books, but that's another story entirely.

The book, *A History of the Seven Seas*, detailed an old sailor's tale about the ancient Sea Hag living on Broken Skull Island. Legend had it The Sea Hag had one of the biggest collections of magical trinkets in the world. Rumors said the Sea Hag possessed eerie magical powers, and nobody left Broken Skull Island without the Sea Hag placing some horrible curse upon them.

It just so happened the *Crusty Claw* was due to pass Broken Skull Island the next morning. Bart figured this was his chance. If he could steal some of the Sea Hag's treasure, he would earn his pirate name and become famous. The next morning, Old Peg Leg agreed to let Bart take a small boat to Broken Skull Island and wait for his return, at least until sundown.

Bart set foot on the swampy ground of Broken Skull Island. The nasty smell of garbage and rotten food made him gag. It was worse than Old Peg Leg's socks, but not quite as bad as Dog Breath Dirk, who smelled like a rotten egg wrapped up in dirty pair of underwear filled with sauerkraut; it was truly worse than anything imaginable.

Bart almost got sick, but he forced himself to remain calm and find the Sea Hag. He wasn't sure exactly how he was going to steal some treasure, or how he could find the Sea Hag. Bart wasn't particularly good at being sneaky and stealing things, and he wasn't good at finding people on stinky islands amongst scary looking trees.

He didn't give up hope. He headed into the woods trying not to breathe in through his nose to avoid the stench. Wandering through the trees, Bart tripped over a large root sticking up out of the muck. He landed flat on his face in the mud. As he started to pick himself up off the soggy ground, he noticed an unusual hole in the ground under the base of a tree only a few feet away. He crawled over to the hole and peered inside. It was dark and looked to be a tunnel straight into the ground under the gnarled old tree. He heard a faint whisper of someone humming at the other end of the tunnel.

Thinking this person may be able to lead him to the Sea Hag's lair, Bart started climbing through the tunnel on his elbows. Bart crawled for what seemed like forever until he noticed a light shining a few feet away. He stopped and listened. He could hear a woman humming a happy tune at the other end of the tunnel. Bart inched forward a little more. The delicious aroma of roast boar made his mouth water. It was the first pleasant smell he'd had on this horrible island.

Peeking around the corner of the tunnel, Bart saw a petite woman leaning over a large iron kettle atop a smoldering cookfire. She was stirring the kettle with a long wooden spoon, humming to herself.

The woman was dressed in a fine dress the color of an overly ripe watermelon, which dragged the floor. The room looked like a giant had scooped away a big chunk of the earth. The walls were dirt and stone covered in thick emerald green moss.

It was a roomy space, filled with hundreds of interesting trinkets stacked in every corner of the room. Bart saw bottles, skulls, animal furs, twisted pieces of metal, knots of rope and twine, and piles of books. Yet the room wasn't dirty, or a mess. Everything seemed somehow to be in its place.

As Bart admired the contents of the chamber, a rather large, hairy spider crawled across his right hand and

Bart choked off a startled scream. The woman turned toward the noise.

"Who dares enter the abode of the Sea Hag!" the woman screeched, her voice shrill and squeaky like a bicycle chain that needed grease.

Bart should have been terrified, but he laughed instead. The Sea Hag wasn't ugly and disfigured like the tales he'd read. In fact, she was quite pretty, in an odd way. Her silver hair was straight and finely combed hanging softly on her shoulders and despite her bright sea-foam green eyes and her pale blue skin, the Sea Hag looked perfectly normal.

"What are you laughing at mud clop?" the Sea Hag asked, her fists on her hips.

"I'm sorry ma'am," Bart said, trying to stand up. "You just don't look at all like a Sea Hag." Bart attempted to brush some of the mud and dirt off his shirt and trousers.

"Thank you, I suppose," she said. "But you didn't answer my question. Who are you?"

"My name is Bart Baker ma'am."

The Sea Hag stepped forward. "And why are you here in my home, Bart Baker?"

"I heard marvelous tales about your collection of magical trinkets, and I wanted to see them for myself ma'am," Bart said, figuring honesty, at least mostly honest, was the best choice.

"Well, Bart Baker, I didn't ask for company and who says I have to show you my collection of magical trinkets?" the Sea Hag asked.

"You ask a lot of questions, don't you?" Bart replied, getting slightly angry about the woman's snobby tone.

"You are a brave one, aren't you, sonny?" said the Sea Hag. "I like that. Come in and have a seat." She, motioning him toward a gnarled old stump against the wall.

Bart sat and talked with the Sea Hag for quite some time. He even shared a cup of green lizard soup with her, which surprisingly wasn't bad, and a hunk of roast boar, which was wonderfully tasty. After their meal, the Sea Hag stood quickly.

"Ok, let's get this over with then, Bart Baker," she said.

Bart was puzzled. "What do you mean?"

The Sea Hag shrugged. "I've enjoyed your company, but nobody comes to my island without wanting to take away something that belongs to me. I'm betting you're no different."

"I'm just trying to earn my pirate name," Bart explained. "I don't want any trouble. If I go back to the *Crusty Claw* without something to show for this trip to Broken Skull Island the other pirates will laugh me right off the ship."

"Well, Bart Baker, you are a nice boy, and I wouldn't want to cause you any problems," the Sea Hag said. "I'll come up with some treasure for you to take with you, if you earn it."

Bart's left eyebrow raised. "And how can I earn it, ma'am?"

"Simple, Bart Baker, answer three riddles and I shall give you three items of great magic and you can be on your way."

Bart stood up. "If I can't answer your riddles what happens?"

"First, I'll have to put a nasty curse on you," she said tapping her cheek with her finger. "Then I suppose you'll have to stay here with me and be my slave for a few years. You could leave now with a small curse. What will it be my young friend?"

Jay S. Willis

Chapter Four

Riddles

Bart decided it was worth the risk. He sat back on the stump as the Sea Hag posed her first riddle.

"He has a look of awful scorn

And wears his clothes a funny way,

Waving his hands over fields of corn,

He keeps the birds away!

Who is he?"

Bart's brain began to whirl and churn, as did his stomach. He was nervous now. After a few moments, Bart regained control over himself.

"I can do this," Bart thought to himself.

After several long minutes, the Sea Hag tired of looking at him, but she didn't lose her patience. She began tidying up the dishes from their meal.

"I suppose it's my fault I didn't specify a time limit to our little game, Bart Baker," she said with disappointment. "I'm not as good at this as I used to be. Getting old, I guess. Take your time and remember one wrong answer, and I win the game."

The Sea Hag began humming the same tune she was humming when Bart first found the entrance to the cave.

Bart turned the words over in his mind for quite some time. Corn and birds. Corn and birds. Suddenly, he had a flash of inspiration. Birds liked to eat corn, but that wasn't good for the corn. Farmers put a scarecrow in the field to stop the birds from coming.

"I've got it, ma'am," Bart said proudly. "He's a scarecrow."

The Sea Hag turned toward Bart with a slight smile. "Very good, Bart Baker, you are correct, but that was the easy question. They get harder."

As she dusted a bookshelf in the corner, the Sea Hag began reciting the second riddle:

"I have holes on the top and bottom.

I have holes on my left and on my right.

And I have holes in the middle, yet I

still hold water.

What am I?"

She was right, this one was a bit tougher it seemed, but Bart was gaining confidence now. After several minutes, Bart realized he needed to focus on water. He was a sailor. Nay, he was a pirate! He should know the answer to this. What could possibly have holes in it and still hold water?

A bucket with holes in it lost all the water if not plugged up. Ships had portholes, but never holes in the middle. They'd sink. Wiping up the hold of a sinking boat was no fun. The *Crusty Claw* had sprung a leak before and they all had to pitch in, mopping the floor up with sponges tied to sticks.

Sponges.

"That's it!" Bart said in surprise.

"What's it, dear?" said the Sea Hag without looking up from her sweeping.

"I have the answer, ma'am," said Bart. "A sponge. I know from experience."

"That's correct my young friend," she said. "Now, for the most difficult of the three riddles. Remember, if you lose, you'll have to be my slave."

"I went into the woods and got it.

I sat down to seek it.

I brought it home with me because I couldn't find it.

What is it?"

This one would take some serious thought he realized. He wasn't a woodsman. He'd never been comfortable in the woods. What did you go into the woods to find? Animals? Berries? No, that wasn't it. What could you bring home with you because you couldn't find it? Bart was confused and becoming worried. He started losing his confidence.

"Here, try this dear," said the Sea Hag handing Bart a wooden cup of steaming liquid. "This will help you think."

Bart sipped at the tea for a while. He ran his finger around the rim of the cup as he pondered the riddle. Nothing was coming to him this time. He began to think all hope was lost.

Just then, he felt a sharp little pain in his finger. It felt as though something bit him. He'd had his finger on the rim of the cup. Bart looked at his finger and found a small bit of wood sticking out. A splinter.

"Wait a minute," Bart thought to himself. You could get a splinter in the woods. If you sat down to find it, but didn't, you could take it home with you, without having found it. He had the third answer.

"I've got it, ma'am," Bart said with a big toothy smile.

"And what would you have, my dear?" the Sea Hag asked.

"The answer to your riddle," Bart replied. "Do I get to pick the treasure, or do you?"

The Sea Hag smiled. "You're slick little one, I'll pick the treasure. Now, what's your answer?"

"A splinter," he said, thrilled at his triumph.

The Sea Hag nodded her head. "Congratulations, my boy! You are gifted," she said, walking around the room looking for something.

"I'll live up to my word, Bart Baker, but you must understand there is still a price I forgot to mention," said the Sea Hag.

Bart cringed. "What's that?" he asked.

"If you want to back out now, I'll let you go free of charge, otherwise you have to pay the price to leave the island," she replied.

Chapter Five

Treasure

"I'll take my chances," Bart said boldly.

She continued scrounging around the room for a few moments. Bart sat patiently trying to pick the splinter out of his finger. He got the splinter free when the Sea Hag stepped in front of him with a small chest in her hands.

The Sea Hag reached out her hand and carefully fastened a small pendant to Bart's sleeve. The pendant was two black gems trimmed in a shiny gold, one triangular, the other cut in a circle. Bart had never seen anything like it before.

"This is the Dream Pendant," the Sea Hag said. "If you wear it or hold it in your sleep it will protect you from magic affecting your dreams. It wards off nightmares and makes sure you have happy dreams."

Bart nodded. "Thank you."

Second, the Sea Hag placed a small item in Bart's right hand. "This is the Crystal Ball of Jabuz," she explained. "The claws are carved like the Dragonmen of Drakken. The crystal is powerful."

Indeed, he held a long gold necklace which held a pair of carved silver dragon-like claws clutching a tiny crystal ball.

She sat down on the stump next to Bart to finish her explanation.

"The Crystal Ball is sometimes called the Wishing Crystal. It holds powerful magic, which grants the owner three wishes. However, you must be careful with your wishes. The first rule is that you cannot wish harm to anyone in any way. The second rule is that your wish will only come true if you are pure of heart. The third rule is that if your wish does come true, it will come true sometime in your lifetime, maybe not immediately. Finally, you must give the Crystal to someone deserving of its magic after you have used your three wishes. That is why I am giving it to you, Bart Baker."

Bart was astounded. This was a truly magnificent and powerful piece of magic. He didn't know what to say. Before he could respond, the Sea Hag placed a third item in his hand. A small, silvered ring with a pearl set in between two rectangular pieces of cut sapphire.

"This is the Ring of SHHHH!" she said. "This ring will protect you from all evil monsters as long as you wear it and are still. You cannot make any sound while you wear it, or its magic will not work. If you are quiet, then no bad monsters can see you, or harm you in any way."

"Thank you very much," Bart said. "I suppose I should leave you now. I must get back to my ship."

The Sea Hag stepped in front of Bart. "Not so fast, dear," she said with a sly look on her face. "You have to pay the price to leave my island."

The Sea Hag whispered a few words Bart didn't understand, sprinkled some sort of light blue powder, the color of a robin's egg, over his head and gave him an unexpected kiss on the lips.

"There you go my friend," she said crossing her arms as she stepped aside. "That wasn't too painful now was it?"

Bart was amazed. He didn't feel any different.

The Sea Hag pointed toward a short doorway opposite the tunnel where he had entered. "If you'd like to leave the civilized way this time," she said with a smile.

He walked toward the door and turned before he left. "Thank you again, ma'am. I've enjoyed your company."

The Sea Hag continued smiling and nodded. "Come back and see me again, Bart Baker. I would be glad for the company. I must say you're the most pleasant pirate I've ever encountered."

Bart opened the door to find he was stepping out of the trunk of an incredibly old, exceptionally large tree. He saw the sun was near setting. Bart scrambled toward the beach.

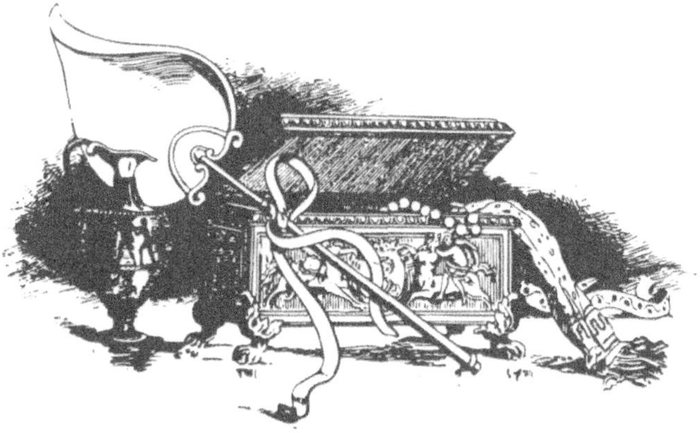

Chapter Six

Pirate Name

As the *Crusty Claw* started pulling up anchor, Bart rowed aside the ship. He was glad to be back aboard.

After washing himself and changing clothes, Bart found Old Peg Leg on deck watching the waves go by.

"So, did you find the Sea Hag, my boy," Old Peg Leg asked with a hand on Bart's shoulder.

Bart smiled.

Old Peg Leg looked shocked and took a few steps back. "What happened to you on that island, boy? You're not sick, are you?"

"What do you mean?" Bart asked.

"Your front teeth are all pitch-black boy, black as night," Old Peg Leg answered.

Bart pulled a small hand mirror from his coat pocket. Indeed, the Sea Hag had placed a curse on him. His teeth were now black.

"I suppose it could be worse," Bart said with a shrug.

"Well, are you going to tell me, or not?" Old Peg Leg asked impatiently.

Bart saw no reason to lie. However, the truth wasn't all that exciting as far as pirate adventures go. He told Old Peg Leg the absolute truth and showed him his three treasures.

Old Peg Leg clapped Bart on the shoulder. "That's a good story boy, but what happened with that old Sea Hag anyway?"

Old Peg Leg didn't believe him. Bart didn't know what to say. He had told the truth.

"I know, you found her, you knocked the old hag over the head, took her by surprise, and stole those three trinkets of hers, right?" Old Peg Leg asked.

"No, it happened like I said," Bart replied. "And she was actually a nice lady."

"A good one, boy," Old Peg Leg chortled loudly. "Let's see, did you find her cave, set fire to her and those three things were the only treasure you could save from the fire?" Old Peg Leg asked. "Yeah, that sounds like it to me, that's what really happened, right? You're being humble."

Bart shrugged. "No, I'm telling you the truth."

"Well, to sneak up on the Sea Hag and set her cave on fire to steal some of her magic trinkets you deserve your pirate name, boy," Old Peg Leg exclaimed.

"I know, we'll call you Blacktooth from now on," he said triumphantly. "Blacktooth Bart."

Bart never thought he'd be disappointed when he got his pirate name, but he was. From that day forward, everybody called him Blacktooth. Every pirate on the Seven Seas exaggerated the story of his adventure on Broken Skull Island terribly and he became famous. Blacktooth learned that not every story was true. Often, the truth about things was simple and not necessarily exciting.

Eventually, the nickname Blacktooth Bart became Blacktooth the Pirate. It was a more formal title with more respect added to it since his adventure was so grand in the minds of all the other pirates. Old Peg Leg retired and Blacktooth bought the *Crusty Claw* from him. For several years, Blacktooth and his crew sailed the Seven Seas having many grand pirate adventures.

Chapter Seven

Blacktooth's Treasure Chest

Unfortunately, it now seemed as though Blacktooth's adventures were at an end. Blacktooth had been named Pirate of the Year when his crew won The Great Pirate Challenge. Dog Breath Dirk believed Blacktooth cheated when in fact he hadn't.

Nonetheless, Dog Breath Dirk chased down Blacktooth and his crew and managed to sink the *Crusty Claw* with a few well-placed cannon balls to the hull of the ship. Blacktooth had always heard that little fishes in the sea needed to be careful because there was always a bigger fish to be worried about who might eat you. He never thought about that until he saw Dog Breath Dirk's huge ship, the *Red Razor*, coming after him. Dog Breath's ship was at least twice the size of the *Crusty Claw*. Now, Blacktooth knew to beware because there is always a bigger ship out there waiting for you.

After several weeks shipwrecked on the island, Blacktooth finished building a nice little cabin from the hull of his ship. He still had some timbers left over.

To pass the time he carved many little animals and built all kinds of little trinkets. Soon he realized he'd never had a treasure chest. That would be his next project. A treasure chest.

Blacktooth took several days to build his treasure chest. As a well-trained pirate with years of experience, Blacktooth knew that locking things in a chest wasn't the best way to protect your treasure. Locks could be broken.

He intended his treasure chest to be for storage purposes. He had found many items of clothing washed upon on the shore from his ship in the days after the

Crusty Claw sank. The only real treasure Blacktooth had left were the three items he had gained from his meeting with the Sea Hag on Broken Skull Island.

Blacktooth decided just in case of emergency he would build a secret compartment in his treasure chest. In the event of emergency, or further attacks by Dog Breath Dirk, he would have a safe hiding place for his three most prized possessions. If nothing else, he had to make sure they were left in the right hands, or at least not discovered by somebody like Dog Breath Dirk.

Blacktooth took the hinges off the armoire of the Queen of Zithromaz. He managed to scrape most of the pink off, but found it was an impossible task. No matter how hard he tried, there would still be some pink on those hinges.

Blacktooth did manage to find a few boards from the inside of the pink dresser that were not in fact pink. Those, he used in his chest only to find that he had missed cutting one board correctly and it still bore the word "queen" inscribed on it, as did every board and piece of wood in the armoire.

On the day Blacktooth finished building his treasure chest, he saw a frightening sight in the distance. Dog Breath Dirk's ship was coming near. He had finished the chest in time. Blacktooth did not dare take a chance on his treasure being discovered or taken from him by Dog Breath Dirk. In the wrong hands, such a thing could be disastrous.

Blacktooth knew what he had to do. He placed the Wishing Crystal in his hand. Gripping it tightly, he made his third and final wish. His first two wishes had come true already, but that's another story.

Blacktooth wished he would make his way to safety and somebody pure of heart and mind, who would not misuse, or abuse their powers, would find his three treasures.

Blacktooth immediately placed his treasure in the secret compartment of the chest. He placed the small lock on the compartment door and made sure it was locked securely. He hoped Dog Breath's men would not be smart enough to find the secret compartment.

As the lock snapped into place, the entire chest began to glow a faint blue. Blacktooth assumed that meant his wish had been granted. Most likely, a magic spell had imbued the chest to prevent anybody not pure of heart and mind from opening the secret compartment. At least, that's what he thought.

Just as Dog Breath's men landed, Blacktooth began to float off the ground slowly. A fluffy blue cloud formed under his feet and in a great whoosh, magically transported Blacktooth off the island.

Of course, where Blacktooth ended up, and what happened to the chest are stories, for another day.

THE END

For now

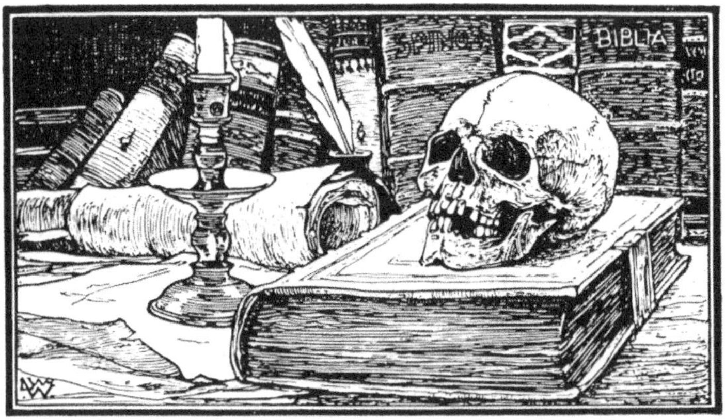
BIBLIA

ABOUT THE AUTHOR

JAY S. WILLIS

"My goal as an author is to create an engaging and fun body of work to sustain a generation through their life as readers of Fantasy: from intelligent chapter books to sprawling epics."

From an early age, Jay was fascinated by story-telling and wrote his first books in grade school by hand using typing paper packets stapled together for him by his mother. An avid Dungeons & Dragons role-player, growing up in the 80's obsessed with Star Wars and Raiders of the Lost Ark, Jay's reading and writing interests have always skewed toward the fantasy and science-fiction genres.

Jay S. Willis is a graduate of both Capital University and Capital University Law School. Jay has been a licensed attorney for 25 years.

Please follow Jay online at www.jayswillis.net and on Facebook at https://www.facebook.com/atlaslawauthor.

For exclusive news and content join Jay's Mailing List at https://www.jayswillis.net/newsletter-signup/. All Subscribers get a FREE copy of *The Sphere Saga* Novella *The Magic of Justice and Revenge*.

Thanks for reading about Blacktooth! Jay would really appreciate it if you could leave a Review of this book!

Acknowledgements

Thank you first and foremost to my family. Sharing bedtime stories with my children served as the inspiration for Blacktooth the Pirate. While I loved reading to my kids when they were little, I also found myself creating my own stories to entertain them and Blacktooth came to life. He belongs to my kids, but it's time we shared him with the world. It's the right thing to do.

Thanks to Duketranart for the amazing cover illustration!

Thank you to Jason Lovins for helping with cover layout and design.

Thanks to Thomas J. Hamilton for editing assistance.

Jay S. Willis

SNEAK PEEK

Blacktooth and the Legend of Skull Mountain

Long before Dog Breath Dirk marooned Blacktooth the Pirate, sinking the *Crusty Claw*, Blacktooth and his band of pirates sailed the seas in search of the fabled treasure of Skull Mountain. This should in no way be confused with Broken Skull Island where Blacktooth encountered the Sea Hag who cursed him changing his teeth black from whence he derived his pirate name. In pirate circles, skulls are particularly important and many things in life happen to be associated with them.

Blacktooth was always a polite and gentlemanly pirate. While he was generally feared the world over, he was known as the Friendly Pirate as well. Folks traveling by ship always hoped if their ship were boarded by pirates, it would be Blacktooth aboard the *Crusty Claw*.

Traveling the Caribbean near Port Seabreeze one foggy morning, Blacktooth's lookout, Eagle Eye Ernie, spotted a cruise ship off the port bow. The crew of the *Crusty Claw* hadn't boarded any ships lately.

"Follow that ship," Blacktooth said to Helmet Henry the helmsman.

As the *Crusty Claw* approached the cruise liner, Eagle Eye Ernie yelled down from the crow's nest, "Captain, it's the Caribbean Queen we're approaching."

Blacktooth smiled. "Ah, my good friend Captain Gavin, I'm sure we'll all eat well tonight," he said to his First Mate Jumpin' Jimbo Jiminy who smacked his lips and rubbed his big belly. "I hope they're having shrimp tonight, Captain. I love the Caribbean Queen's shrimp scampi," Jumpin' Jimbo said.

Blacktooth patted the First Mate on the shoulder, "Not as much as Eagle-eye Ernie. Sounds good doesn't it. We'll find out shortly," he said.

As the *Crusty Claw* came up gently beside the ocean liner, Captain Gavin stood on deck waiting for Blacktooth with a smile.

PLEASE HELP KEEP BLACKTOOTH SAILING!
LEAVE A REVIEW OF THIS BOOK ON AMAZON!

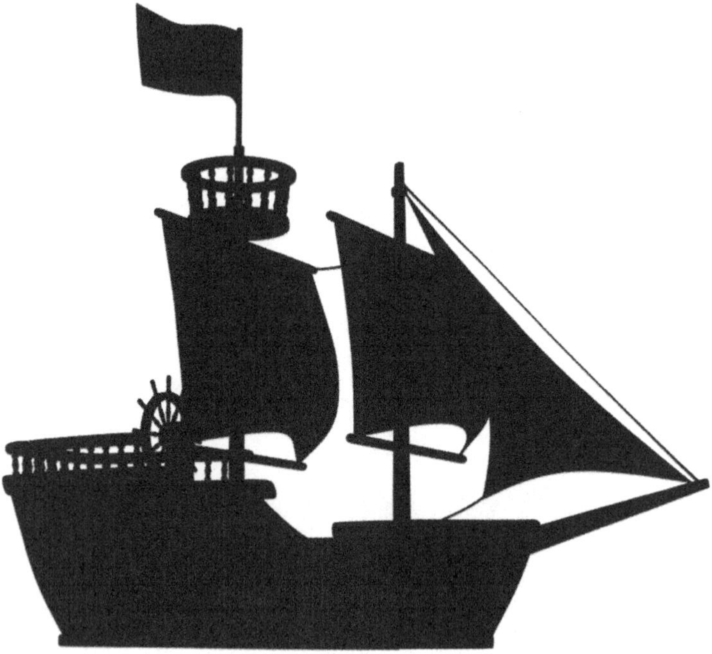

Books by The Author

Blacktooth and the Legend of Skull Mountain

Pirate life may be perilous, but it's probably different than you'd think. Blacktooth is a friendly pirate. He enjoys reading, eating, and searching for treasure with his crew. *The Adventures of Blacktooth the Pirate* recounts what it's really like to be a pirate.

Blacktooth's high-seas adventures are fun for kids of all ages and reading doesn't have to be like walking the plank.

In *Blacktooth and the Legend of Skull Mountain*, our friendly pirate captain gains a treasure map marking the location of the fabled treasure of Skull Mountain. After Blacktooth visits his favorite library to research the legend, he and the crew of the *Crusty Claw* discover Skull Mountain, but the treasure has a dangerous guardian and won't be easy to plunder.

Can you guess what perils await Blacktooth the Pirate on Skull Mountain?

Blacktooth and The Great Pirate Challenge

Pirate life may be perilous, but it's probably different than you'd think. Blacktooth is a friendly pirate. He enjoys reading, eating, and searching for treasure with his crew. *The Adventures of Blacktooth the Pirate* recounts what it's really like to be a pirate.

Blacktooth's high-seas adventures are fun for kids of all ages and reading doesn't have to be like walking the plank.

Blacktooth and The Great Pirate Challenge is perhaps his most exciting adventure yet. Blacktooth and his crew compete for the Pirate of the Year title in a crazy contest full of misadventures with Dog Breath Dirk cheating and trying to sink the *Crusty Claw*.

Will Blacktooth become Pirate of the Year? Why does Funalota Island have three queens? How many shrimps can one pirate eat?

Blood is Thicker than Magic

The Arcana Chronicles: Volume 1

An ancient family feud. Strange magic. Can one uncertain boy heal an eldritch rift?

Thirteen-year-old Daniel Waldera is struggling with life's changes. Realizing he has feelings for his best friend is hard enough, and the idea of confessing them to her is even more terrifying. But when he's attacked by an evil spirit and turns a flashlight into a lightsaber to vanquish it, the young teen faces a whole new level of confusion.

Discovering he's heir to powers from both his grandfather and his dad, Daniel finds himself caught in the middle of a long-running family rivalry. And with his best friend afraid of his growing abilities, fulfilling a prophecy is the last thing he wants.

Can Daniel defeat his own fears in time to become the master of magic he was born to be?

Blood is Thicker than Magic is the page-turning first book in The Arcana Chronicles Middle Grade/Teen urban fantasy series. If you like everyday heroes, unexpected destiny, and coming-of-age adventures, then you'll love Jay S. Willis's riveting tale.

Buy Blood is Thicker than Magic to settle a mystical dispute today!

The Heart of Magic
The Arcana Chronicles: Volume 2
Forthcoming Fall 20223

When a should-be nemesis becomes his brother-in-arms, will this powerful magic-user lead his team to triumph or succumb to a knife in the back?

World War II. Aaron Kinney is eager to do his duty. Focused on learning from his assigned mentor, the young soldier is shocked to hear his bunkmate is a member of a rival magical faction. But he's willing to set aside their traditional feud in exchange for help tracking down a Nazi necromancer spreading rot across America's heartland.

Digging into the world of formidable mystical artifacts, Aaron and his clever companions try to snare the German mastermind before he can construct a dangerous device. And though they celebrate every small victory, their enemy's dark powers seem to keep him perpetually one step ahead of the plucky group.

Will old jealousies ruin their only chance at defeating an army of the undead?

The Heart of Magic is the action-packed second book in The Arcana Chronicles middle grade/teen urban fantasy series. If you like determined heroes, exciting spy stories, and worlds full of wonder, then you'll love Jay S. Willis' alternate history.

Buy *The Heart of Magic* to put the corpses back in the grave today!

Dream of the Sphere
The Sphere Saga: Book 1

Three thousand years of tradition torn asunder. When the truth comes out, will a hero emerge to pick up the pieces?

Dashira Eisenheart takes ultimate comfort in her community. So she's thrilled when her brother ascends to the coveted order chosen to protect the world from safely sealed-away, millennia-old, dangerous magic. But her faith in her beloved parents' loyalty cracks after she spies her mother sneaking about town to meet with the enemy.

Striving to stay focused on her own academic studies, Dashira becomes caught in family tensions that soon reach a boiling point. And as her father's Brotherhood and her mother's rebel group head toward a cataclysmic clash, the young seeker finds herself trapped by conflicting choices.

Will she face her fears and accept her role in a grand destiny?

Dream of the Sphere is the intricate first entry in the expansive The Sphere Saga epic fantasy series. If you like gargantuan conflicts, jaw-dropping twists, and deep explorations of humanity's beliefs, you'll love Jay S. Willis' hard-hitting tale.

Buy *Dream of the Sphere* to wake a giant today!

Dawn of the Sphere

The Sphere Saga: Book 2

Thousands of years ago, magic ruled their land. When the mightiest among them rise up, will they bring peace... or rain down destruction?

Axamar Sulvastra discovered his powers on the day his brother died. Instead of saving a life, his accidental outburst robbed him of something truly precious. And now he fears the Red Rage pumping through his veins could either free the world or send it to its doom.

Working hard to control his abilities at the Academy of Arcane Studies, Axamar quickly bonds with two other gifted and potent mages. But as jealousies erupt and unchecked power festers, their irreparable discord could cost them everything when a devastating plague threatens to ravage the planet.

Can Axamar unite The Three to repair the realm before all life is obliterated?

Set three millennia before the events of book one, *Dawn of the Sphere* is the second book in the immersive The Sphere Saga epic fantasy series. If you like complex interpersonal intrigue, powerful backstories, and blockbuster battles, you'll love Jay S. Willis' mind-blowing origin story.

Buy *Dawn of the Sphere* to see how it began today!

War of the Sphere
The Sphere Saga: Book 3

The lines have been drawn. The battle for the realm has begun. Can this young woman become the leader who can stop the spread of evil?

Dashira Eisenheart never planned to head a rebellion. But when three millennia of magic suppression end to unleash devastating forces upon the world, she launches into a fight for her people. And every day the war over the Sphere-Blessed continues to rage, the closer her homeland edges toward utter annihilation.

Struggling to control her own abilities and teaming up with The All-powerful Three, Dashira hunts for magical artifacts to swing the conflict in their favor. But a dangerous trek reveals shocking secrets about the nature of reality that could tear apart the very fabric of time.

Can this rebel warrior save the future before the present is ground to dust?

War of the Sphere is the thrilling conclusion to the groundbreaking The Sphere Saga epic fantasy series. If you like deep worlds, intricate characters, and vivid depictions of all-out combat, then you'll love Jay S. Willis' mind-altering story.

Buy *War of the Sphere* to bring home victory today!

Order of the Sphere
The Sphere Saga: Book 4

With the brutal conflict finally over, their magical skills have been restored. But can they survive a full-scale battle for the future?

Arstal Axamar hopes for a new dawn of peace. With the war ended, the decorated veteran travels the land to survey the havoc caused by the ending of eons of magic suppression. But he's horrified to discover that nature itself has been warped, releasing terrifying creatures of legend and allowing the return of a demented ancient enemy.

Motivated by the fear of losing everything they've worked for, Arstal tries to free a trapped ancestor who could be the key to victory. But with his allies bracing for a devastating invasion without the protection of the Sphere, his realm may be racing toward oblivion.

Can this brave soldier win the fight to save his people from extinction?

Order of the Sphere is the exhilarating fourth book in the epic fantasy The Sphere Saga. If you like loyal leaders, detailed worlds, and tales of bravery above all else, then you'll love Jay S. Willis' titanic adventure.

Made in the USA
Las Vegas, NV
29 August 2025